W9-ATT-572

24638

JF
HUR

Hurwitz, Johanna

"E" is for Elisa

$12.88

DATE			
WITHDRAWN			

BAKER & TAYLOR

Renbrook
School

The Alan N. Houghton Library

WITH LOVE FROM
THE GRANDPARENTS' GROUP

"E" IS FOR ELISA

By Johanna Hurwitz

Johanna Hurwitz
"E" IS FOR ELISA

Illustrated by Lillian Hoban

Alan N. Houghton Library
Redbrook School
2028 Albany Avenue
West Hartford, CT 06117

Morrow Junior Books
New York

Text copyright © 1991 by Johanna Hurwitz

Illustrations copyright © 1991 by Lillian Hoban

All rights reserved. No part of this book may be reproduced or utilized in any form or by any means, electronic or mechanical, including photocopying, recording or by any information storage and retrieval system, without permission in writing from the Publisher. Inquiries should be addressed to William Morrow and Company, Inc., 1350 Avenue of the Americas, New York, N.Y. 10019.

Printed in the United States of America.
2 3 4 5 6 7 8 9 10
Library of Congress Cataloging-in-Publication Data
Hurwitz, Johanna.
"E" is for Elisa / Johanna Hurwitz : illustrated by Lillian Hoban.
p.   cm.
Summary: Four-year-old Elisa gets her picture taken, starts learning to read, breaks her arm, and experiences other exciting aspects of growing up.
ISBN 0-688-10439-8 (trade) — ISBN 0-688-10440-1 (library)
[1. Family life—Fiction.] I. Hoban, Lillian, ill. II. Title.
PZ7.H9574Eaar   1991
[Fic]—dc20   91-159   CIP   AC

"E" is for
Everyone in the Adler family:
Renée, David, Michael,
Eddie, and Eitan

Contents

Tears and Frowns

Elisa Michaels was four years old. She lived in an apartment house in New York City with her parents and her big brother, Russell. Russell was eight years old, which was very grown-up. But every day, Elisa was getting more grown-up, too. Her biggest wish was to catch up with Russell.

1

These days, Elisa was old enough to go to the Sunshine Nursery School. That made her feel happy and proud. Still, even though she was happy most of the time, it seemed as if rarely a day went by without at least a few tears running down Elisa's cheeks.

"She's a crybaby," grumbled Russell.

"Everyone cries sometimes," said his mother. "I cried when I watched a sad movie on television last night. And just yesterday, you cried when you broke the model of the dinosaur that you were building."

"Yeah," Russell admitted reluctantly. "But Elisa cries all the time."

Elisa cried when she discovered that her favorite red shirt was in the laundry and she couldn't wear it to school. Elisa cried when the box of cereal was empty and she had to have toast for breakfast instead. She cried when she fell in the playground, and she cried when her balloon broke at the zoo. Elisa cried when Rus-

sell found a nickel on the sidewalk and she didn't.

"Crybaby. Crybaby. Elisa is a crybaby," taunted Russell.

Russell's words always made Elisa cry even more. She didn't like it when Russell teased her.

"Stop that, Russell," said Mrs. Michaels. "When you were her age, you had awful tantrums."

"What are tantrums?" Elisa wanted to know.

"Tantrums are loud crying and kicking and yelling. They are not very nice."

Neither Russell nor Elisa could remember the tantrums. "I don't believe it," said Russell. "You're just making it up."

"Elisa," said her mother, "if you can't wear your red shirt today, it means you can wear it tomorrow. If the cereal is all gone, it means I will be buying a big new box of it."

Elisa blew her nose and nodded her head.

4

She knew her mother was right. It was silly to cry about her red shirt. But sometimes she couldn't help it. The tears just popped out of her eyes. And whenever they did, Russell teased her.

"Crybaby! Crybaby!" he would say.

It always made Elisa cry even harder.

Sometimes when Elisa was home from nursery school, she liked to look at the family photo album. It was filled with many, many pictures. Elisa liked to see pictures of Russell when he was a baby. It was hard to imagine that her big brother had once been so small. She tried to imagine what it was like when Russell had one of his tantrums.

There were many pictures of Elisa, too.

"Where is my hair?" she asked, pointing to one of her pictures.

"You were bald for a long time," said Mrs. Michaels, laughing.

5

Elisa ran her fingers through her hair and tried to remember what it felt like to be bald. She could not remember it at all.

As she turned the pages, Elisa found it interesting to see the changes. Gradually, she had grown hair and gotten bigger. Russell had gotten bigger, too. The newer pictures looked more and more the way she appeared when she saw herself in the bathroom mirror nowadays.

Mrs. Michaels pointed to a picture. "Do you remember that pretty party dress you used to have?" she asked.

Elisa shook her head. She could not remember ever having a pink dress with ruffles.

"You used to call them *russells*," said Mrs. Michaels.

Elisa laughed. She could not remember being so little and so silly.

"I have an idea," said her mother. "It's going to be Grandma's birthday in a couple of weeks. I'll take you and Russell to a profes-

6

sional photographer and have a new picture made of the two of you together. It will make a wonderful present for Grandma."

"Will there be flashbulbs?" asked Elisa. She hated flashbulbs. The bright, sudden light always made her eyes feel funny.

"Maybe," said Mrs. Michaels. "But the flash is over in an instant."

Elisa frowned. She didn't want to have her picture taken even if the flash was over so fast.

"You're such a big girl now," said Mrs. Michaels. "The photographer will take a picture of you and Russell, one-two-three. And it will make Grandma so happy."

Elisa tried to think of Grandma looking happy, but still she felt her eyes filling with tears.

"What dress would you like to wear?" asked Mrs. Michaels. "You could wear your blue corduroy jumper or the green plaid dress."

"Green," said Elisa.

So on the Saturday morning when they had

an appointment with the photographer, Elisa put on her green plaid dress. She had a matching green ribbon in her hair. Russell wore slacks and a jacket. He had a shirt and a necktie on, too. He looked very grown-up.

"I don't think Grandma ever saw you in a tie, Russell," said Mrs. Michaels. "She will just love this present."

"Airmail wants to be in the picture, too," said Elisa, picking up the rag doll that her grandmother had made and sent especially for her.

Russell made a face. But he didn't say anything.

The photographer's name was Mr. Gottlieb. He took them into a brightly lit room. "You sit right there, sweetheart," he said to Elisa. He pointed to a bench.

"Now, you will stand right beside her, young man," he said to Russell.

Elisa frowned as she looked around for the camera. Was there going to be a flashbulb?

She had a funny feeling that even though she wanted to smile and look happy, she might start crying. She hoped she was wrong. Grandma wouldn't like a picture of her crying. She sat Airmail on her lap so Grandma would see her.

"Why don't you leave your doll over here?" asked Mr. Gottlieb, pointing to a table in the corner.

"Yeah," said Russell. "That's a good idea."

"No," said Elisa, and her eyes filled with tears.

"I don't mind the doll being in the picture," said Mrs. Michaels. "Elisa can hold her."

Mr. Gottlieb shrugged his shoulders and stood back. He looked at the children. He came forward and adjusted Russell's necktie a bit.

Mrs. Michaels stood off to one side. She waved to Russell and Elisa. "Don't forget to say cheese," she said, smiling at them.

9

Mr. Gottlieb picked up his camera and focused it. "All ready?" he said. "Cheese."

Neither Russell nor Elisa wanted to say *cheese*. That was a stupid thing to say just because they were getting their picture taken.

Elisa took a deep breath and held on tightly to her doll. She forced her lips into a smile. Mr. Gottlieb pushed the shutter button on the camera and a bright light flashed.

Elisa blinked her eyes.

"Don't move," said Mr. Gottlieb. "If you don't like cheese, say chocolate."

Russell scratched his nose and Elisa closed her eyes as Mr. Gottlieb pushed the shutter again.

"Russell, you moved," Mrs. Michaels called out. She hadn't noticed that Elisa had closed her eyes.

"Say chocolate cheese," the photographer called out. The flashbulb on the camera went off once again. Again, Elisa's eyes were closed.

This time, Mrs. Michaels noticed and so did

Mr. Gottlieb. "Don't shut your eyes, sweetheart," he called to her.

"I can't help it," Elisa whined softly.

"Sure you can. It just takes a moment." The flashbulb exploded once again and Elisa's eyes blinked shut. Tears began to trickle down her cheeks. "I want to go home," she said.

"We're almost finished, dear," said Mrs. Michaels. She rushed forward and wiped Elisa's eyes with a tissue. "Just a little smile for Grandma," she begged.

Elisa sniffed back her tears and tried to smile at her mother. "That's the way," said Mrs. Michaels.

"Crybaby. Crybaby," Russell said, taunting her.

"I am not," said Elisa. But the tears began to come down her cheeks again.

"Russell, stop that at once," Mrs. Michaels scolded her son.

Mr. Gottlieb opened a drawer in a desk and pulled out a hand puppet. "Look at my friend

Coco," he said, putting the puppet on his hand.

"That's for babies," said Russell.

Elisa stared hard at the puppet and tried to smile.

In all, a dozen shots were taken of Elisa in her green plaid dress and green hair ribbon and Russell in his jacket and necktie. "I'm sure at least a couple will be winners," said Mr. Gottlieb as they left his studio. "They'll be ready for you on Tuesday."

On Tuesday when Elisa came home from the Sunshine Nursery School, her mother showed her the photographs. Russell stood tall and handsome in all the pictures except the one where he was scratching his nose. Airmail's eyes and smile were sewn onto her cloth face, so her expression was the same in each picture. Elisa's green plaid dress and her matching hair ribbon looked beautiful. But in all the pictures except one, Elisa's eyes were

12

tightly shut. In the one where her eyes were open, she looked terrified.

"You look as if a lion was going to attack you," said Russell.

"You look as if you were afraid of Mr. Gottlieb," said Mrs. Michaels.

"You look like you saw a ghost," said Russell.

"You don't look very happy," said Mrs. Michaels.

"I can't help it," said Elisa.

In the end, they sent Grandma not one, but two pictures. One picture was Russell standing tall and handsome in his jacket and necktie. It was half of one of the photographs that Mr. Gottlieb took.

The other present was a self-portrait of Elisa, which she had drawn with her colored markers. It didn't look exactly like Elisa, but the girl in the picture was wearing a green plaid dress and a green hair ribbon. Her eyes

14

were wide open and she was smiling. She was holding a rag doll named Airmail.

"Maybe next year, we'll be able to send Grandma a photograph of you, too," said Mrs. Michaels hopefully.

"Maybe," said Elisa, smiling. Next year was a long way off.

Elisa's Secret

Elisa had a secret. It was very tiny, and it fit inside her pocket. It was the best secret she ever had, and she couldn't wait until she took it home.

The secret was a tooth. The tooth used to belong to Stephanie Loomis. Stephanie was a student in Elisa's class at the Sunshine Nursery School. She was six months older than Elisa, and much bigger than her, too. That morning when the children arrived at school, Stephanie showed everyone that one of her bottom teeth was loose. She sat jiggling it. Elisa came to watch.

She looked at Stephanie's fingers, which made the tooth wiggle back and forth.

"I wish I had a loose tooth, too," she told her classmate.

"Do you want to touch my tooth?" Stephanie offered.

Elisa could not believe her good luck. Carefully, she held out her fingers and wiggled Stephanie's tooth.

"Elisa, Stephanie, what are you doing?" the teacher asked, coming toward the two girls.

Elisa jerked her hand out of Stephanie's mouth, and the li'tle tooth came away in her fingers. She could hardly believe what she had done. She hadn't meant to pull out Stephanie's tooth. It was an accident.

17

"I was just checking Stephanie's tooth," Elisa said softly to the teacher. "I didn't know it would come out."

"Look," said Stephanie, grinning. She poked her tongue in the hole where the tooth had been a moment before.

Elisa was relieved that Stephanie didn't seem at all angry as she took the tiny white tooth from Elisa. Elisa knew she wouldn't want anyone to pull a tooth out of *her* mouth.

All the children came to look.

"Put the tooth in your pocket," said the teacher, after everyone had had a chance to admire it. Outside Stephanie's mouth, the tooth looked more like a tiny white pebble than a tooth that had once chewed her food.

"You're a lucky stiff," said Justin.

"Put it under your pillow tonight," said Annie Chu.

"The tooth fairy will come and take it," said Vanessa.

All the children knew about the tooth fairy.

During art time that morning, while the children made collages using macaroni and buttons and sticky glue, Elisa thought about Stephanie's tooth.

During juice and cookie time, Elisa thought about Stephanie's tooth, too. She wished she had a little tooth to stick under her pillow for the tooth fairy. Elisa knew a lot of people who had put teeth under their pillows. Her brother, Russell, had lost many of his baby teeth. So had her friends Nora and Teddy. Annie Chu hadn't lost a tooth yet, but one was a tiny bit loose. Elisa wondered if she would ever have a tooth to put under her pillow. It made her feel like a baby to still have every single one of her baby teeth. She didn't have one that was even a teeny-tiny bit loose.

At dismissal, when the children were getting their jackets from the cubbies, Stephanie put her hand inside her pocket and pulled out her tooth to admire it again.

Suddenly, Elisa had an idea. "I'll trade you something for your tooth," she offered.

"What?" asked Stephanie, looking interested.

"I have a quarter in my bank at home," she said.

Stephanie considered. "The tooth fairy would give me a quarter, too," she said. "What could you trade me that's different?"

Elisa thought hard. At home she had a lot of toys, but if she didn't give Stephanie something right now, it would be too late.

"Do you want my mittens?" she offered. She pulled them out of the pockets of her jacket. They were hand-knitted by her grandmother. One mitten had a little girl's face on it. The other had the face of a boy.

"Okay," said Stephanie. And in a moment, the mittens were hers. In exchange, Elisa took the little tooth. She put it inside the deep

pocket of her overalls so it wouldn't get lost. And she decided not to tell her mother about it when she was picked up. It would be a secret!

Elisa had never had such a tiny secret before. It was so tiny she could hardly feel it inside her pocket. But at the same time, the secret was so big that it filled her whole head. All during her lunch of chicken noodle soup, she kept thinking about the tooth.

"You're very quiet today," commented Mrs. Michaels to her daughter. "Did you have a good time at school?"

Elisa chewed up the noodles in her mouth and nodded her head. "We made collages and I got sticky glue all over my fingers," she said. "But I peeled it all off." She showed her mother her fingers, which were free of glue. She did not show her the tooth in her pocket. And she did not tell her about it, either. If she told her mother about the tooth, it would not be a secret anymore.

Elisa decided not to put the tooth under her pillow until the evening. It was fun to put her hand deep into her pocket and feel the little tooth hiding there. But when Russell came home from school, she almost forgot and showed it to him.

Russell always brought home so many important-looking papers. He had arithmetic worksheets with red checks, he had spelling tests, he had drawings. Tomorrow, when all the sticky glue had dried, Elisa would be able to bring home her collage. But today, she had the little tooth inside her pocket. Although she couldn't show it to Russell, it was good to know it was there.

After school, Russell went to his Cub Scouts meeting. Mrs. Michaels took Elisa to the park. When she was riding on her tricycle, her fingers got cold. But when she put her hands into her pockets to get her mittens, they weren't there. Stephanie had them.

Elisa didn't care if her fingers were cold. It

was much better to have the little tooth to hide for the tooth fairy than to have her mittens. She rode holding on with only one hand and put the other hand in her pocket to keep warm. After a bit, she changed hands so the other hand could have a turn inside a pocket.

"Where are your mittens?" called Mrs. Michaels from the park bench where she was sitting and talking with the other mothers.

"I don't have them," said Elisa. It was true, but it was only part of the truth. Elisa was glad that Stephanie didn't live nearby. If she had come to the park wearing Elisa's mittens, then her mother would have learned about the trade and the secret.

At supper, Russell talked all about the Cub Scouts. They were going to have a cookout on Saturday. They were going to bake potatoes and make hamburgers outdoors in a big park in New Jersey.

"That's just like what we're eating now,"

said Mrs. Michaels. It was true that they were having hamburgers and baked potatoes for supper. But everyone knew it tasted different if you cooked the foods outdoors and ate them outdoors, too.

At any other time, Elisa would have felt sad. She wished she could be a Cub Scout and go on Saturday trips. Today, because she had her secret inside her pocket, she felt happy. She just poured more ketchup on her hamburger and kept on eating. Soon it would be bedtime, and she would put the little tooth under her pillow.

"How was your day, Elisa?" asked Mr. Michaels. "Do you have anything to report?"

"Stephanie's tooth came out in school," Elisa said. The words fell out of her mouth even faster than the tooth had come from Stephanie's mouth.

"Did she bleed?" asked Russell.

"No," said Elisa. She was sorry that she had mentioned the tooth. Maybe the secret would

25

fly out of her mouth next if she wasn't very careful.

"When I lost my front teeth in nursery school, I bled," said Russell, sounding very important.

"Do you still remember that?" asked his mother.

"Yes," said Russell. But mostly he remembered hearing his mother talk about it. It had happened a long time ago.

When Elisa was getting undressed for her bath, she slipped the little tooth out of her pocket and under her pillow. Then she put her overalls into the laundry hamper. It would have been funny if she forgot and the tooth got washed in the washing machine. It would be like getting a super toothbrushing, only without using a toothbrush.

Elisa kissed her parents good-night and got into bed. She couldn't wait to fall asleep and wake up in the morning. Then she would see what the tooth fairy had brought her.

"What are you smiling about?" her mother asked. "You've been so quiet all day. But I guess it was a good day if you're smiling."

"It was a good day," said Elisa. "And tomorrow will be a good day, too." She was thinking about waking up and getting a surprise even though it wasn't her birthday.

However, the next morning when Elisa woke up, she forgot about the tooth. Her father had already left the house, and Elisa was in the middle of eating her bowl of cereal when she suddenly remembered. She jumped off the kitchen chair and ran back into the bedroom. She slid her hand under the pillow to feel for the surprise that the tooth fairy left.

What a surprise. The tooth fairy had left the tooth.

Elisa burst into tears. She went back into the kitchen. "The tooth fairy didn't come here last night," she said, as the tears dripped down her cheeks. She held out her hand to show her mother the little tooth she was holding.

"When did your tooth fall out?" asked Russell.

"Open your mouth. Why didn't I notice?" asked Mrs. Michaels.

Elisa opened her mouth, but there was no space to show a missing tooth. "This is Stephanie's tooth. I traded for it so I could have a tooth for the tooth fairy."

"Well, no wonder the tooth fairy didn't come," said Mrs. Michaels, hugging her daughter. "I bet the tooth fairy went to Stephanie's house last night looking for that tooth."

"But it wasn't there," said Elisa.

"Exactly," said Mrs. Michaels. "The poor tooth fairy must be very confused. Why in the world would the tooth fairy expect to find Stephanie's tooth at our house?"

"It's not Stephanie's tooth anymore," protested Elisa. "She traded it to me. So now it is mine."

"Maybe so," said Mrs. Michaels. "But I

don't think tooth fairies bring gifts for teeth that didn't fall out of your own mouth."

"I didn't know that," said Elisa sadly. "I wouldn't have traded my mittens to Stephanie."

It was time to get ready for school. Elisa kept her hands in her pockets all the way there. At school, Stephanie announced that she had gotten a quarter under her pillow from the tooth fairy. It was really magic how the tooth fairy knew about the missing tooth even though it wasn't under Stephanie's pillow.

Later in the day, Elisa still didn't have any loose teeth. Russell laughed when his mother told his father what Elisa had done.

Mr. Michaels didn't laugh. "Be patient," he told Elisa. "You'll have plenty of your own loose teeth before you know it."

Even without losing a tooth, Elisa got a surprise. Two mornings later, she found her old mittens under her pillow. One mitten had the face of a little girl. The other mitten had the face of a boy. They were the mittens she had traded to Stephanie in exchange for her tooth.

"The tooth fairy must have been worried that your hands were getting cold," said Mrs. Michaels.

The tooth fairy was awfully nice.

A Day of Snow

Late one winter afternoon, it began to snow. Elisa hugged her father when he returned home from work. His heavy coat was wet from melted snowflakes.

"I hope the snow sticks," said Russell.

He ran to the window to look out into the street. Elisa followed to look, too. The sky was dark but the street was lighted by the lamps along the block. The snow sparkled as it flew through the circles of light cast by the street-lamps. On the ground, Elisa could see foot-prints where people had walked in the fresh snow. New snow was quickly filling in the tracks.

"It's sticking! It's sticking!" Russell shouted with delight.

"It's sticking! It's sticking!" echoed Elisa.

After supper, both Russell and Elisa checked on the snow. It was coming down even heavier than before. The branches on the little trees along the street were covered with the snow. The cars parked along the curb were almost hidden now. They looked like small white mountains.

"I love snow," said Russell. "I hope it never stops!"

Elisa tried hard to remember last winter, when she had played in snow. But she had been much littler then, and she couldn't recall

33

that long ago. Even without remembering, she was sure that she loved snow, too.

Just like Russell, she said, "I hope it never stops." She held Airmail up to the window so that she could admire the snow outside.

The snow did not stop. It continued falling while Russell and Elisa were sleeping. In the morning, it was still falling—and outside the window the world was white and quiet.

"This is the most snow I ever saw," said Russell with awe. "It will be fun to walk to school."

"I think school will be closed today," Mrs. Michaels said. She turned on the radio in the kitchen as the children ate their breakfast.

"How could school be closed?" asked Russell. "It's not Saturday or Sunday, and it's not a holiday. It's just a plain old Friday."

Before his mother could explain that occasionally a heavy snowstorm brought about school closings, the radio announcer interrupted the music that had been playing.

34

"Here is a news bulletin that has just come in," he said. "Due to the sixteen inches of snow, all city schools will be closed today." He began to list other institutions that would be closed, but no one at the Michaels's house heard another word the announcer said.

"Yippee!" shouted Russell. "There's no school!"

"Yippee!" shouted Elisa. "There's no school!"

"I thought you both liked school," said Mr. Michaels to his children.

"I like school when there is no snow. But I *love* snow," said Russell.

"Me, too," said Elisa.

"Can I go out and play in the snow right now?" Russell asked.

"Me, too?" asked Elisa.

"Sure," said their father. "I'm going out to play in the snow, too. We'll all go."

"You?" both Russell and Elisa asked their father at the same time.

"Daddies don't play," said Elisa.

"You have to go to work and make money," Russell reminded his father.

"If you can stay home today, so can I." Mr. Michaels laughed. "Besides, I don't expect the buses or subways to be running very well in all this snow. The whole city is going to be closed today."

"Yippee!" said Elisa. It would be fun to play in the snow with her father and Russell.

Before going outside, they had an awful lot of clothing to put on. On top of Elisa's regular corduroy slacks and polo shirt went a sweater, snow pants, woolen scarf, snow jacket, boots, and a woolen cap. Then, after the snow jacket was zipped up, Elisa's mother pulled the hood of the jacket over the cap. Finally, Elisa put on her mittens.

The whole family got into the elevator together. Elisa carried her blue plastic bucket and shovel, which she used to dig in the sandbox in the park in warm weather.

Russell didn't bring his pail and shovel. "Pails and shovels are for babies," he said. "I'm going to make snowballs."

"I can make snowballs *and* dig in the snow, too," said Elisa. "Are we going to the park?" she asked her parents.

"We don't need the park today," said her mother. "Besides, with all this snow, you won't be able to find your sandbox."

"Or the benches," said Mr. Michaels.

"Or the park," said Russell.

It was strange to think of the whole big park hidden under snow. But outside, their street was indeed hidden. You could not tell where the sidewalk ended and the street began. All was covered by the heavy snowfall except for tiny, narrow paths. The janitors of the buildings had been out early, shoveling these paths and clearing the steps leading into the houses.

Their street had never seemed so clean or so still. Puffs of steam escaped from their mouths as they stood in the cold air, listening to the

unexpected quiet and admiring all the bright-
ness of the white around them.

"Look," said Russell. "There are no cars!"

Sure enough, the broad avenue near their
home was completely empty of traffic. There
were no car horns beeping or motors running.
That was why it was so quiet.

"I never saw the street without cars on it,"
said Russell.

Then the most amazing thing happened:
Mr. and Mrs. Michaels and Russell and Elisa
began walking in the middle of the street.
They didn't watch for a green light, and they
didn't worry about cars and buses and trucks
coming.

Russell and Elisa made many tracks where
no one had yet walked. Their feet sank into the
snow, making deep holes. It was a lot of fun.
From one building, a man came out to walk his
dog. The dog sniffed at the snow suspiciously
and walked cautiously along one of the paths.
But then they saw another dog that seemed to

love the snow as much as they did. The dog was jumping into the cold white stuff and digging in it with its paws.

Gradually more and more children and grown-ups came out of the neighboring buildings. The adults were enjoying the snow as much as the children.

Mr. Michaels made a snowball and threw it at Mrs. Michaels. Then she made one and threw it at him. Russell made a snowball and threw it at his father. But Elisa hid behind a white mountain that used to be a car. The balls of snow flying through the air frightened her. She didn't want anyone to throw a snowball at her.

Soon several of the older children were throwing snowballs at one another. They all laughed and thought it was fun. Elisa trudged through the snow back toward the entrance to their building, where she felt safer. She loved the clean white snow, but she didn't want anyone to throw a snowball at her.

"Elisa," said her father, "why don't you dig with your shovel over here?" He pointed to a spot near the front of the building.

Elisa began to dig.

"Hi, Elisa," a voice called out. It was Nora Resnick, who lived in the same building. "Let's make a snowman together," suggested Nora. Even though she was older than Russell, Nora had brought a shovel outside to play with.

"First we have to make a big pile of snow, and then we pack it together so it doesn't fall apart," said Nora. She seemed to know all about snow and snowmen.

Elisa dug up snow and added it to the pile that Nora was making. "I like snow but I don't like snowballs," said Elisa.

"Snowballs are fun when the snow is soft and clean like this," said Nora. "But making a snowman is more fun, isn't it?"

Elisa nodded in agreement.

Soon they had a big mound of snow. Several

other children came and wanted to help, too. There was Nora's brother Teddy and another boy named Josh. Elisa saw her friend Annie Chu. Eugene Spencer, who lived in the same apartment building as Elisa, was there, also. He was bigger than any of the others, so he helped make the snowman's head. Now that so many children were digging in the snow, Russell came over to join them.

"I wish I had brought my shovel outside," he said. But since he didn't have it with him, he used his mittened hands for digging.

The snowman grew much taller than Elisa. He was taller than Russell, too.

"Now we have to find something for his nose," said Eugene Spencer.

Elisa knew just what they needed. She had seen pictures of snowmen in her library books. Within minutes, she went up and then down in the elevator of the building with her mother. She returned holding items that she had gotten in their kitchen: a big carrot for the nose, plus two round chocolate cookies to use for eyes.

Eugene Spencer put them all in place. "Too bad he doesn't have a hat," he said. "It's so cold outside today, this snowman sure could use one."

Elisa thought hard. "I know what we could use," she said. She held up her blue plastic pail. "He could wear this."

Eugene Spencer took the pail and put it on top of the snowman's head.

"That's a silly thing for a hat," said Russell. He was sorry that it wasn't his red pail that was on top of the snowman's head.

Now that the snowman was completed, everyone began to feel the cold, even through all their clothing. It was time to go inside and warm up.

After a hot lunch, Elisa wanted to go outside and play in the snow again. It was no longer snowing. Already everything looked very different from the morning. There were wider

paths on the sidewalk, and a snowplow had cleared the avenue. Although it moved slowly, there was traffic once again on all the streets. Some cars and trucks had chains on their tires. They made a funny rattling sound.

One of the snowman's eyes was missing. Perhaps someone had eaten it. Or maybe it had fallen onto the ground and been buried in the snow.

"By tomorrow, things will return to normal," said Mrs. Michaels. "Everything will be open and running as usual."

"But not school. Tomorrow is Saturday," Elisa said joyfully. She could tell that there was certainly enough snow to last for a whole white weekend. And she had a feeling that Russell was going to bring out his pail and shovel and dig with her.

The Bathing Suit

In Florida, where Elisa and Russell's grandparents lived, it was as hot as summer all
year long. Their grandparents could go swim-
ming even in the wintertime. That was why,
even though it was February, Elisa's grandmother mailed her a new bathing suit. "I
found this on sale," her grandmother wrote

46

on a small card. "I know it will be perfect for Elisa."

The card was inside a box that held a bright red bathing suit with white polka dots.

"I want to wear it right now!" Elisa insisted when she saw the bathing suit. It was the prettiest bathing suit she had ever seen.

"You can try it on now," said her mother. "But it's much too cold to wear a bathing suit in February. You will wear it in the summer when we go to the beach."

Elisa pulled off all her clothes and climbed into the bathing suit. "It's just the right size," said Elisa as she ran to admire herself in the mirror. Then she danced around the apartment in the red bathing suit with the white polka dots. "I want to wear it to school tomorrow," she said.

"School! Nobody wears bathing suits to school," said Russell, laughing at his little sister's demand.

"Be patient," said her mother. "We'll put

the bathing suit away. Before you know it, summer will be here."

That was the silliest thing Elisa had ever heard. There was still loads of dirty snow along the curbs out on the street. It wouldn't be summer until all the snow melted, and that would take ages and ages.

Elisa's eyes filled with tears. How could she wait so long until summertime?

"Crybaby." Russell began to tease her.

"It's not fair," said Elisa. Russell had gotten a new sweater in the package from their grandmother. He wouldn't have to wait until summer to wear it. He could wear it right now.

Mrs. Michaels put the bathing suit in Elisa's drawer with her underwear. "You can peek at your bathing suit whenever you want," said her mother. "And it will wait here until the weather gets warm."

Before she went to bed that night, Elisa checked to be sure her bathing suit was still safe in the drawer. It was. Elisa pulled the bathing suit out and put it under her pillow. That way she didn't have to worry about it getting lost in the nighttime.

The next morning, Elisa awoke early. She often woke up before Russell and her parents. Usually, she stayed in bed and whispered secrets to Airmail. But this morning, Elisa remembered the bathing suit under her pillow. She decided to try it on again. Very quietly, so as not to awaken Russell, Elisa got out of bed. She took off her pajamas and climbed into the bathing suit again. Elisa rubbed the shiny fabric and admired it once more. It was the best bathing suit in the world.

She sat on her bed and pretended that she was at the beach. In a way, it was like being at the beach because whenever they went there, they sat on a blanket. But at the beach there was sand, too. Elisa wished she had some sand in her bed so it would really be like the beach.

She thought about sand. What did they have in the house that she could use for pretend sand?

Elisa thought about all the things that were in the house. Salt was a little like sand. But there wouldn't be enough salt inside the salt shaker. Then she had a wonderful idea. She knew what would be perfect!

Tiptoeing from the bedroom very quietly, Elisa went to the kitchen. Underneath the sink, Mrs. Michaels kept a big box of laundry detergent. Like salt, it was white, so it was the wrong color. But it was in teeny-tiny pieces, and it felt a little bit like sand. Best of all, there was plenty of it in the box.

Elisa took the box back to her bedroom. She poured detergent all over her bed. Then she sat down on her blanket again. Something was missing. She thought for a minute, and then she got out of bed again. On the shelf where she kept her toys were her blue plastic pail and shovel. In good weather, she used them when she played in the sandbox in the park. Just last week, she had used the pail and shovel to dig in the snow. Now she could dig in the sand on her bed.

She began filling the pail with the detergent that was all around her. Suddenly Elisa's nose began to tickle. She sneezed once. Then she sneezed a second and a third time. Even though she was happy playing in her bed, she felt little tears coming into her eyes.

Russell turned over in his bed. "Are you catching a cold?" he asked Elisa.

"No," said Elisa. "I don't feel sick." She sneezed again.

"Why are you wearing your bathing suit?" asked Russell, looking at his sister. "It's too cold to wear it now."

"I'm not cold," Elisa insisted. She sneezed two more times in quick succession. "I'm playing that I'm at the beach," said Elisa.

Russell got out of bed to investigate. "What is this?" he asked, fingering the white powder that covered Elisa's bed.

"Sand."

"Sand?" said Russell. He sneezed.

"Are you getting a cold?" asked Elisa.

"Maybe I'm catching it from you," said Russell. "What kind of sand is this?" he asked, studying Elisa's bed.

"It's soap sand!" said Elisa, giggling, but a sneeze burst out of her together with the words.

"Soap sand!" exclaimed Russell, laughing. He filled his fists with the white grains and tossed them into the air. "Now it is soap snow," he said as the tiny bits of soap fell, landing on Elisa and her bed.

Mr. Michaels walked into the bedroom. "What's going on in here?" he asked. "Elisa, what are you doing in your bathing suit at this hour? And at this time of year?"

Elisa sneezed. "I just wanted to wear it

again," she said. She sneezed two more times in a row.

Mr. Michaels grabbed the blanket to wrap around his daughter. As he did so, soap powder fell from the blanket and onto the floor. "What is this?" asked Mr. Michaels. He gave a very loud sneeze.

"It's soap sand," Russell reported. He sneezed, too.

"I'm pretending it's sand," said Elisa. "I was playing that I was at the beach."

Mr. Michaels bent down and picked up the box of laundry detergent, which was half under Elisa's bed. "What is this soap doing here in your bedroom?" he asked.

"I told you. I made a beach in my bed," Elisa explained. She rubbed her nose, which was feeling so tickly. And she blinked her eyes. They were feeling itchy.

"Beaches belong near the ocean," Mr. Michaels said. "Not in bedrooms. And soap powder belongs in a washing machine and not in a bed."

Tears filled Elisa's eyes. "I want to wear my bathing suit at the beach *now*," she said. "I don't want to wait until it's summertime."

"Crybaby. Crybaby." Russell began to taunt his sister. But he started sneezing and that interrupted his words.

"Stop that at once, Russell," said his father. "Elisa is disappointed that she can't wear her bathing suit now. There is no reason for you to tease her."

Mr. Michaels might have said more on the subject, but he began to sneeze. "This soap is making us all sneeze," he said. "And it's making my eyes tear, too. Get some clothing on quickly," he told the children. "Then, Elisa, you can shovel all the soap back into the box for me. We'll need it when we do the next batch of laundry."

At that moment, Mrs. Michaels came into

the bedroom. She stared in amazement at the sight before her. There was Elisa sitting in her bed, wearing her bathing suit and surrounded by soap powder.

"What is this?" she asked.

Mr. Michaels explained it all to his wife.

Elisa thought her mother might be angry that she had borrowed her soap powder. But to her surprise, Mrs. Michaels began laughing.

"I've never seen anything so funny," she said, choking out the words between bursts of laughter. Tears began to stream down Mrs. Michaels's face. Then Mr. Michaels started laughing, and that made Russell and Elisa laugh, too.

"Why are you crying?" Elisa asked when she noticed her mother's tears.

"These are tears from laughing," said Mrs. Michaels. "This is the funniest thing I've ever seen," she said.

Reluctantly, Elisa removed her bathing suit. Summer was such a long time off. She could look at her red bathing suit with the white polka dots, but she couldn't wear it till days and days and weeks and weeks passed.

As she got dressed that morning, Elisa had a second good idea. She put on a pair of underpants and a long-sleeved turtleneck shirt. Over the shirt, she put on her bathing suit. Then she pulled on a pair of slacks. You couldn't see all of the bathing suit, but the top half of it showed just fine. And she wouldn't have to worry about being cold during the day, either.

"Look at me!" She showed her mother proudly when she went into the kitchen for breakfast.

"She's wearing her bathing suit!" protested Russell. "Nobody wears a bathing suit in the middle of the winter."

"I do!" said Elisa.

"It's going to be a lot of trouble taking it off whenever you need to go to the bathroom," warned Mrs. Michaels.

"I don't care," said Elisa. "I can do it."

And she did. All that day, Elisa wore her new bathing suit. Nobody would have even known it was a bathing suit, except that she told everyone. She told her teacher at nursery school. She opened her jacket to show the new bathing suit to Nora and Teddy Resnick when she met them in the elevator. She even opened her jacket and showed off the bathing suit to the woman who worked behind the counter at the bakery when she went with her mother to buy some fresh bread that afternoon.

In the evening, Elisa took off the bathing suit and put it in the laundry hamper. It was funny to think that it was going to be washed with the soap sand.

After it was laundered, the red bathing suit with white polka dots was put in the drawer with Elisa's underwear again. And there it stayed until it was really summer and she could wear it to the real beach where there was real sand.

A Smile

Elisa wondered if she would ever be as smart as Russell. Russell seemed to know everything. He knew how to tie his own shoelaces. He knew how to tell time. He knew how to read and write. He knew how to swallow an aspirin without choking. He knew how to work the microwave oven. He knew *everything*.

Sometimes when Russell wasn't busy playing with his friends or going to Cub Scouts meetings or doing his homework or reading his library books, he played school with Elisa. Russell was the teacher and Elisa was the student. Elisa liked it when Russell taught her new things. That way she could learn as much as he knew.

Elisa already knew all the letters of the alphabet. The first letter she had learned was E, because E was for Elisa. But now she knew them all: A B C D E F G H I J K L M N O P Q R S T U V W X Y Z.

Elisa had thought that once she could recognize every letter she would know how to read, just like Russell. But reading was much harder than that. Every word had a different combination of letters. Some words were little and some words were big.

When Russell was younger, he had been given a set of letters that were magnetic on the back. The letters stuck to the refrigerator.

Elisa thought they stuck by magic, but Russell explained that it was because of the magnets. One day Russell took the letters **E-L-I-S-A** and showed Elisa her name. Then he took an **M** and showed her that **M** was for Michaels. She was Elisa M.

"I am Russell M.," Russell said. He pushed the letters around on the refrigerator door and showed her his name. Elisa was surprised that even though E was for Elisa, Russell took the **E** to put in his name, too. It made her angry, just a little. E was *her* letter. He shouldn't take it.

"That's the way letters are," Russell explained. "You use them over and over. Some letters are used a lot. E is a very important letter. It's a vowel."

Elisa didn't know what a vowel was, but she was proud that the first letter of her name was important.

Russell looked around on the refrigerator door and found another **E** to put back in Elisa's name. It was lucky that his set of letters included two of everything. But then he took both the **L** and the **S** from Elisa's name to finish up **RUSSELL**. It was very confusing that the letters didn't hold still.

While Russell was showing Elisa the letters on the refrigerator door, Mrs. Michaels was in the kitchen, too. She was cutting up apples and making a huge pot of applesauce. When the applesauce was finished and cooling and the whole apartment had a delicious apple-cinnamon smell, Mrs. Michaels got some sheets of clean paper.

"Let's make a big set of letters with this paper," she said to Russell. "Then it will be easier for you to teach Elisa."

Mrs. Michaels folded the paper into small boxes. She took a scissors and began cutting out the boxes until the table was covered with small pieces of paper. Russell helped her.

Next, Russell and his mother wrote a different letter on each piece of paper.

Elisa stood watching them. "Make lots of Es," she urged them. "E is one of the most important letters there is."

Mrs. Michaels wrote the letter **E** on five different little pieces of paper.

Elisa beamed with pleasure. E for Elisa was a very important letter.

Soon the table was covered with every letter of the alphabet: **A B C D E F G H I J K L M N O P Q R S T U V W X Y Z**.

"Let's show Elisa some words that she says every day," suggested Mrs. Michaels.

"Do my name first," said Elisa. That was the most important word of all.

So Russell picked out the letters and spelled out **ELISA** on the table. Then, because there were enough letters, he could spell his name, too.

"This is what **MOMMY** looks like," said Mrs. Michaels. "And here's **DADDY**, too."

When it was time to set the table for supper, Mrs. Michaels found a box to put all the little

letters in. "Now you can play this game whenever you want," she said.

Since Russell was so busy playing with his friends, going to Cub Scouts meetings, doing his homework, and reading his library books, he could not play school with Elisa and teach her new words with the letters every day. But sometimes, in the evening, when Elisa was bathed and in pajamas, there would be a little time for one short game with the letters. Every time they took out the little papers, Elisa insisted that the first word they made should be **ELISA**.

Russell showed her more and more words. He made **NORA** and **TEDDY**, the names of their neighbors. Elisa hadn't known that Teddy had an E in his name, too. Russell made the words **HOUSE** and **STREET** and **AIRMAIL** and **MICHAELS**. Some evenings, if they had enough time before bed, the whole table was covered with words. Elisa loved playing with the pieces of paper. She was beginning to understand about the same letters being used over and over again. Russell made Elisa look at the words in their library books. He showed her how the same letters were repeated. He told her about big letters and little letters, too. But Elisa liked big letters better. "E" looked more important than "e."

"Do you remember this word?" Russell asked his sister.

Elisa looked. **RUSSELL**. "It's *Russell!*" she shouted with recognition. "It's your name."

"Right!" said Russell.

Elisa shouted, "I can read! I can read your name."

"What's this word?" asked Russell. Elisa looked. **MOMMY**.

"That's *Michaels!*" she shouted with delight.

"Wrong," said Russell. "It's Mommy, silly. Michaels and Mommy both start with an M, but they are different words."

Elisa didn't like to be called silly. "Don't call me silly," she said. "Show me some more words."

Russell looked through the letters to make another word.

"Time for bed," Elisa's father called.

"Already?" complained Elisa. How could she learn new words if she had to go to sleep?

"What does *sleep* look like?" asked Elisa.

Russell pushed the letters around. **SLEEP**. "There are three letters from **SLEEP** in **ELISA**," Russell noted.

"That doesn't mean I want to go to sleep," said Elisa firmly.

"I never want to go to sleep," Russell agreed. He looked at the letters on the table. "Hey, look at this," he said. He pushed together the letters **ELISA M**. "If you take these letters from your name and move them around, you can make another whole word," he said. "I never noticed it before."

"What is it?" asked Elisa suspiciously. She

understood that you used the same letters over and over again when you did reading and writing. But she wasn't sure she wanted to share her letters with just any old word.

"ELISA M has the same letters as A SMILE."

"A smile?" asked Elisa, surprised.

"That's right," said Russell. He was pleased with his discovery.

"Look," he said to his father, who had come to take Elisa to bed. "ELISA M has all the same letters as A SMILE."

"Why, so it does," said Mr. Michaels. "I never noticed that before." He smiled down at Elisa. "I would say that's good luck."

"It's better to be a smile than a sneeze," said Russell.

"It's better to be a smile than cheese," giggled Elisa.

"Not if you're a mouse," said Russell. "If you are a mouse, you like cheese more than anything in the world."

"The photographer told us to say *cheese* when he wanted us to smile," Elisa recalled.

"Maybe he thought we were mice," said Russell, laughing.

Elisa tried to imagine a family of mice posing for a picture. It made her giggle.

"Stop wasting time," said Mr. Michaels. "It's time for bed."

And even though Elisa didn't really want to go to bed, she didn't argue. "Okay," she said. Tomorrow she would learn some more new words and try more new things. Every day she was getting bigger and smarter. The thought made her smile.

Elisa's Big Jump

In the bedroom that Elisa shared with her brother, Russell, there was a small table and two chairs. These days, Russell complained that they were getting too small for him. But they were still just the right size for his sister. Elisa sat at the table when she drew pictures. She sat at the table and played tea party with her doll, Airmail. She sat at the table and did puzzles.

One afternoon, while Russell was still at school and Elisa was home playing in their room, she climbed onto one of the little chairs to see what it would feel like if she was as tall as Russell. Instead of putting her foot down on the carpeted floor again cautiously, she did something she had never done before. She held her breath and jumped. It was fun. Elisa had seen Russell jumping off the bench in the park and off the first rung on the monkey bars. Now she could jump, too. She climbed up on the chair and jumped off again and again, proud of this new accomplishment.

"Look what I can do," she boasted to Russell when he came home from school. Elisa climbed up on the chair and jumped off.

"Pooh. That's nothing," said Russell. "Let's see you jump off the table."

"That's too high," Elisa protested.

"Not for me," said Russell. "Watch this."

He climbed from the chair up onto the little table and jumped off.

Russell landed with a muffled thud on the carpet. "See," he said proudly. "You're too little to do that."

"I can so do that," said Elisa. She climbed from the chair onto the table, just as Russell had done. She was a tiny bit scared. But she wanted to show Russell that if he could jump off the table, so could she. Elisa held her breath and closed her eyes. One, two, three, jump.

"I did it!" she squealed with delight. "See, I did it." It hadn't been so hard to do after all.

"Yeah, well, that was easy. Let's see you do this." Russell climbed up on his bed. It was just the tiniest bit higher than the table. He jumped off.

"I can do it," said Elisa. There were so many things that Russell could do that she couldn't. But today she could do all these jumps just like him. She climbed up on the bed and closed her

74

eyes. In a second, she was down on the floor and laughing with relief. "I did it! I did it!"

"Well, anyone could do that," said Russell, looking around the room. "I bet you couldn't jump off the chest of drawers."

Elisa turned to look at the chest. It had three drawers and was taller than she was.

"No one could jump off that," she gasped.

"You can't because you're a baby," said Russell. "But I bet I can."

He pushed the table and one of the chairs over near the chest. First he used the chair to help reach the table. Then he stood on the table to reach his foot up onto the chest.

"Look out below," Russell called, and landed with a heavy thud. "See," he said. "I did it."

"I could do it if I wanted to," said Elisa.

"Let's see you do it, then," said Russell.

"I don't feel like it now," said Elisa.

"That's because you can't. You're just a baby."

Elisa felt tears coming into her eyes. She wasn't a baby—she was four years old. And she hated it when Russell teased her.

"Crybaby, crybaby," chanted Russell, seeing Elisa start to cry.

"No, I'm not," shouted Elisa. She climbed onto the little chair and then onto the table. She was going to show Russell that she could do anything that he did.

"Wait a minute," said Russell, as Elisa started to climb from the table onto the chest. "Maybe you better wait till you get as big as I am."

"I'm not a baby," said Elisa. "I'm getting big now."

"I know it," said Russell. "I was just kidding. Come on down." He held out his hand to help her.

"Get out of my way!" Elisa shouted at him. "I am going to jump!"

"No, don't," said Russell, trying to grab his

76

sister. But it was too late. Elisa jumped.

As she fell, she knocked Russell over, and the two of them landed in a heap on the floor. Both of them began crying at once.

"Look what you did," cried Russell, rubbing his head. "It's all your fault."

"It hurts. It hurts," cried Elisa, holding on to her right arm.

Their mother came running into the bedroom. "What's going on here?" she asked.

"We were playing," said Russell. "And we fell."

"What kind of game was this?" asked Mrs. Michaels, looking at the table and chair, which had been moved across the room.

"It was a jumping game," said Russell. "Elisa jumped on me and I hurt my head."

"It wasn't my fault," sobbed Elisa. "You were in my way."

"The bedroom is not a place for jumping," said Mrs. Michaels. She rubbed Russell's

head. "Does it still hurt?" she asked.

"No," said Russell, wiping his tears on his shirt sleeve.

"*I* still hurt," sobbed Elisa. She hurt so much that she couldn't stop crying.

"Where does it hurt?" asked her mother. She rubbed Elisa's head.

"It's my arm."

"She's just crying because she's a baby," said Russell. Now that his head no longer hurt, he was already forgetting that he had been crying himself a minute ago.

"My arm is all hurt," said Elisa, crying louder than ever.

"Crybaby, crybaby," Russell taunted her.

Mrs. Michaels tried to rub Elisa's arm. Elisa let out a loud cry of protest. "That hurts!" she yelled.

"Oh, dear. Maybe you broke something," said Mrs. Michaels.

The rest of the afternoon was spent at the medical center. First a doctor looked at Elisa's

79

arm. Then she was taken to a different room in the center where another doctor took an X ray of her arm. Sure enough, Elisa's arm was broken.

Two hours later when they arrived home, Elisa had her arm in a cast and she was wearing a sling. Her arm still hurt, but she was so proud of the white cast and sling that she was no longer crying.

"Elisa was a very brave girl today," Mrs. Michaels told her husband a short while later as the family sat down to supper. They were eating a pizza that had just been delivered to the apartment because there had been no time to cook any food.

"I was very brave when I jumped from the chest of drawers," said Elisa, chewing a mouthful of pizza. Her mother had cut her slice into bite-size pieces because it was too hard to hold and eat a slice of pizza with only one hand.

"You were *very foolish* when you jumped from the chest of drawers," said her mother. She looked at Russell. "You were foolish, too."

Russell looked down at his plate. He knew he shouldn't have let Elisa jump off the chest of drawers. Even when he was teasing her about it, he knew she was too little. But somehow, he had kept on teasing her anyway.

"I know," he said softly. "I'm sorry, Elisa. I'm sorry that I teased you. And you're not a crybaby, either. Anybody would cry if they broke their arm. Even the President of the United States."

"From now on, I don't want to hear any more about crybabies," Mrs. Michaels said. "I've told you before that everyone cries sometimes. You cried this afternoon when you bumped your head. And I cried when the doctor told me Elisa had broken her arm. Crying is not bad. Jumping off the furniture—that's bad!"

Russell nodded his head.

"I won't jump off the furniture again," Elisa promised.

"Neither will I," said Russell. He made another promise, too. "I won't tease Elisa about crying anymore, either."

"Good," said his father.

"Good," said his mother.

"Goody," said Elisa.

After supper, Elisa permitted Russell to be the first person to sign her cast. He used a blue marker to write the word **RUSSELL**. Then he drew a little smiling face on the cast.

After her parents had each written a message on her cast, too, Elisa thought of something. "I wish Grandma and Grandpa could write on my cast," she said.

"They don't even know you broke your arm," said Russell.

Elisa had an idea. "We could take a picture and send it to them," she said. She was so

proud of her cast she wanted everyone in the world to see it.

"Do we have any film in our camera?" Mrs. Michaels asked her husband.

"There is a roll in it right now," he said. "But if I take your picture, I'll have to use a flashbulb because we're indoors," he reminded Elisa.

Elisa wrinkled her nose in distaste. She really hated flashbulbs. On the other hand, she wanted to show off her new cast to her grandparents.

"Okay," she said. "It's all right to use a flashbulb."

Mr. Michaels went to get the camera. Mrs. Michaels ran for a comb to fix her daughter's hair.

"Don't forget to smile," said Russell as Elisa stood posing for her father.

"Say *cheese*," said Mr. Michaels.

Elisa grinned at him and the flashbulb went off. "I didn't close my eyes!" shouted Elisa. "It wasn't so bad." She was amazed. It must be that her eyes were growing up and didn't mind the flash anymore.

Mr. Michaels took three more pictures of Elisa and two of Russell so that he could finish the roll of film. "I'll drop these off for developing tomorrow," he said.

"Won't Grandma and Grandpa be surprised!" said Elisa.

She had been so busy posing that she had forgotten about the pain in her arm. Now it no longer hurt her at all. Elisa smiled at Russell. "This is the first time I did something you never did," she said, pointing to the cast on her broken arm.

Her father overheard her remark. "Don't worry," he said. "If I know you, it won't be the last, either."

Johanna Hurwitz is the award-winning author of the popular books about Russell and his neighbors, including *Rip-Roaring Russell* (an ALA Notable Book), *Russell Rides Again, Russell Sprouts, Russell and Elisa, Busybody Nora,* and *Superduper Teddy.* She has worked as a children's librarian in school and public libraries in New York City and on Long Island. And she frequently visits schools around the country to talk about books with students, teachers, librarians, and parents. Mrs. Hurwitz and her husband live in Great Neck, New York. They are the parents of two grown children.